BARRY
THE FISH WITH FINGERS
AND THE HAIRY SCARY MONSTER

For Moz

SIMON AND SCHUSTER
First published in Great Britain in 2011
by Simon and Schuster UK Ltd
1st Floor, 222 Gray's Inn Road, London, WC1X 8HB
A CBS Company

Text and illustrations copyright © 2011 Sue Hendra
By Paul Linnet and Sue Hendra

A CIP catalogue record for this book is available
from the British Library upon request

ISBN: 978 1 47118 185 6

Printed in China
1 3 5 7 9 10 8 6 4 2

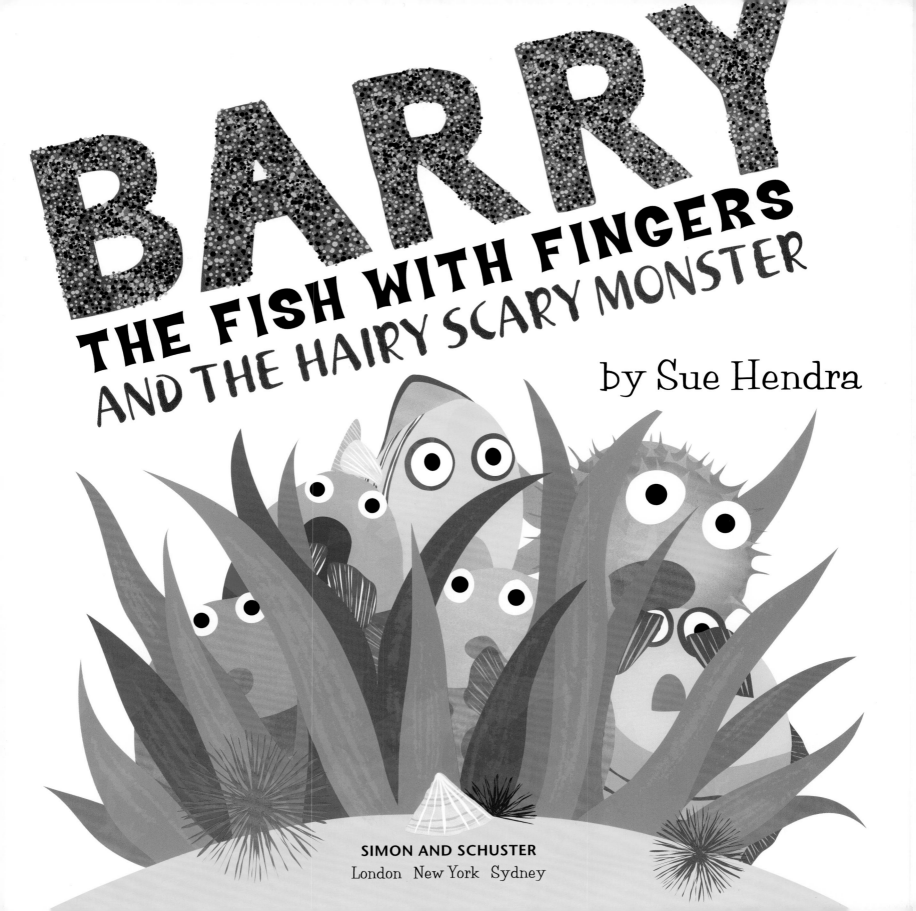

BARRY
THE FISH WITH FINGERS
AND THE HAIRY SCARY MONSTER

by Sue Hendra

SIMON AND SCHUSTER

London   New York   Sydney

Barry the fish with fingers and his friends loved playing hide-and-seek.

Barry was very good at counting.

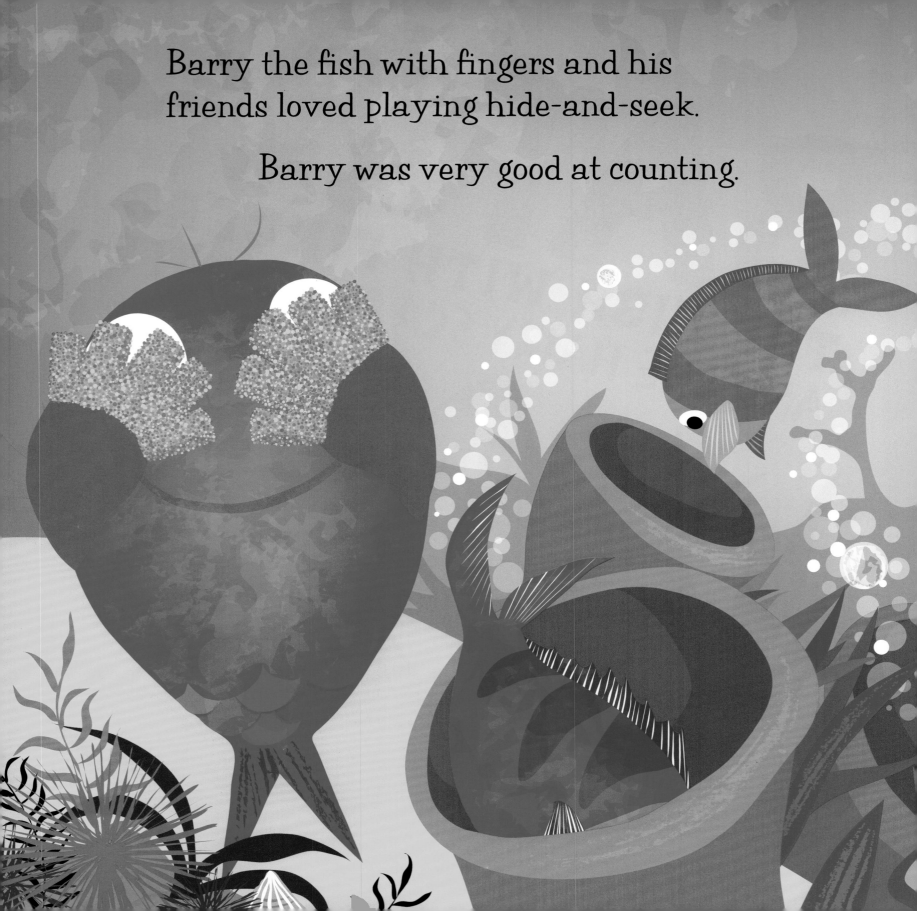

1...2...3...

"Quick!" thought Puffy the puffer fish.
"I need to find somewhere to hide."

But finding a good hiding place wasn't that easy . . .

Too see-through!

Phew, too smelly!

Woah! Definitely too risky!

4 . . . 5 . . . 6 . . .

"Oh, no," cried Puffy.
"Time's running out!"

Then he saw it . . .

"Barry will never find me in here!" he thought.

7...8...9...

10!

"Ready or not, I'm coming!"
yelled Barry.

One by one, Barry found his friends.

BOO!

PEEPO!

FOUND YOU!

But where was Puffy?

Deep inside the wreck, it was dark and scary.
"I hope they find me soon!" said Puffy.
"Eeek! What was that?"

Puffy shot out into the open water.

"Quick, hide or the hairy scary monster will get us!" he yelled to his friends.

The friends huddled together.
"Where's Barry?" asked Puffy.

Oh, no! Barry was missing.

"He must have gone into the wreck
after the monster!" cried Puffy.

Bravely, Barry searched for the monster in every nook and cranny.

Then he heard someone crying.

It was the monster!

"Everyone's scared of me," he sobbed.
"No one EVER wants to play."

Barry smiled. "Don't worry,
I can help you. I know
exactly what to do."

He grabbed a mirror,
a comb, and a pair
of scissors.

Then he set to work.

Snip!

Snip!

His fish fingers moved faster than lightning.

Clip!

Clip!

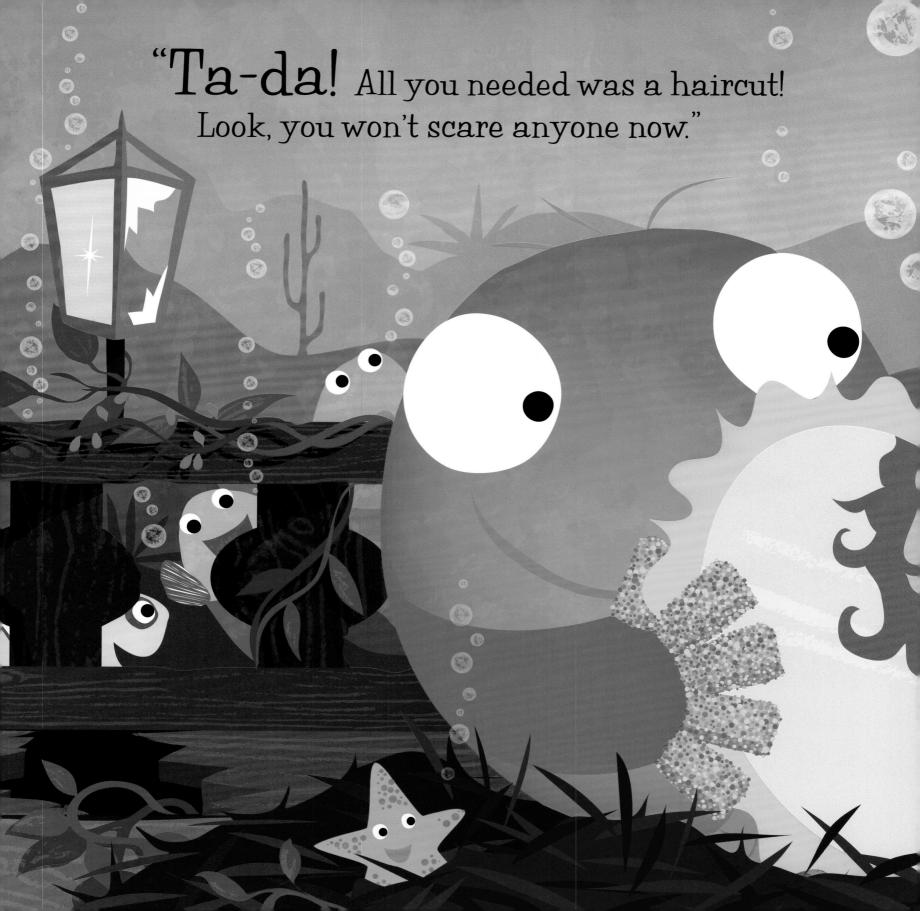

"Ta-da! All you needed was a haircut! Look, you won't scare anyone now."

"Thanks, Barry," Colin the seahorse smiled. "This new haircut is SO me! But what shall we do with all this hair?"

"Easy," said Barry. "Let's all have a 'hair do'!"
So they all had a proper pirate party, and
everyone had the BEST time ever.

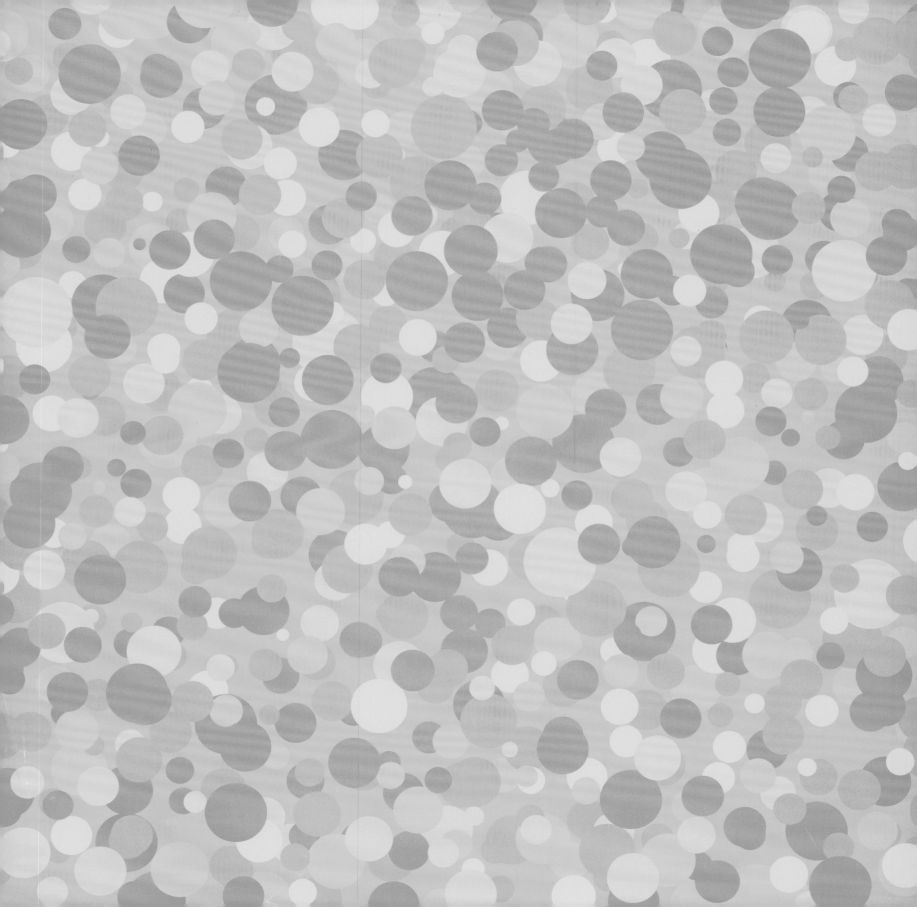